THE
FROG BALLET

Amanda McCardie
with pictures by Caroline Crossland

RED FOX

To my father
A.M.
To Lucy
C.C.

A Red Fox Book

Published by Random House Children's Books
20 Vauxhall Bridge Road, London SW1V 2SA
A division of The Random House Group Ltd
London Melbourne Sydney Auckland
Johannesburg and agencies throughout the world

1 3 5 7 9 10 8 6 4 2

First published in Great Britain by Julia MacRae 1997
Red Fox edition 1999

Printed in Singapore

RANDOM HOUSE UK Limited Reg. No. 954009

ISBN 0 09 187300 2

On midsummer night, the frogs came out of their hiding places. The garden was quiet and cool and the moon was full.

Every night of the year they came out to sing and talk
and play and tell stories, but tonight wasn't quite like other
nights. For some time, the oldest frog had been getting
weaker and weaker. He was now too weak to move far from
the great stone by the lake, and his family wanted to keep
him company. On other nights they would spring across the
grass to play their different games, but tonight they all stayed
close to him.

"What are your favourite colours?" the little speckledy frog asked the oldest frog as they settled down. The favourites game was one they often played together. They usually knew what each other's answers would be, but neither of them minded. To be honest, it was one of the things they liked about it.

"Green and gold," replied the oldest frog without hesitation. "What's your favourite place in the world?"

"This garden," said the little speckledy frog, who had never been anywhere else. "My turn." He gave a little half-hop and fixed the oldest frog with gleaming eyes. "What is your favourite thing to watch?"

The oldest frog pretended to think for a moment. "Moonlight, perhaps."

"Not moonlight!" sang the little speckledy frog, jumping up and running round and round him.

"Spring rains, then. I love spring rains."

"Not spring rains!" shouted the little speckledy frog, throwing himself down again.

"Well then, I think my favourite thing to watch must be ballet."

All the frogs nudged each other and the little speckledy frog fell over. This was the answer he had been waiting for. "Ballet!" he cried, scrambling to his feet again and stretching his arms out wide. "Your favourite thing is ballet! That's why we're going to put on a ballet for you now. The best you ever saw."

The frogs were ready, and they wasted no time.
Two of them swept the great stone by the lake.
Three wove a shining curtain out of spiders' webs.
Four made flutes.

And the little speckledy frog did a bit of sweeping, and
a bit of weaving, and a bit of flute-making, and a lot of
getting in the way.

In between times, he ran over to the oldest frog to check that he wasn't watching when he shouldn't be. The oldest frog was perfectly capable of pretending that his eyes were closed when they weren't, and the little speckledy frog had often needed to be quite stern with him about it. But the oldest frog wasn't cheating tonight.

When the curtain was hanging like a waterfall before
the great stone, the dancers disappeared behind it.

There was a lot of whispering and rustling, then a long,
long pause, and the oldest frog was just dropping off to sleep
when the flute-players began to play.

The curtain rose and the ballet began.

One of the oldest frog's nephews appeared on the stage and began to perform a series of pirouettes. These were spectacular, but they made him dizzy. He caught his arm on the curtain and continued to turn, wrapping himself up so tightly in the process that very soon he couldn't move at all. The music trailed away, he gave a stifled cry, and two of his cousins rushed on stage to unwind him and carry him off.

If the oldest frog was surprised by the turn things were taking, he didn't show it. "Marvellous!" he cried. "Just the thing to make your audience sit up and take notice."

The musicians put down their flutes and clambered on to the stage to hang the curtain up again.

Once it had been put back in position and checked for holes, an animated discussion broke out behind it. The dancers were working out what to do next, and couldn't decide whether or not to risk a repeat performance of their opening solo.

The oldest frog only hoped they would come to a decision before the curtain came adrift again, or someone fell through it.

They must have decided against repeating the pirouettes, for when the curtain rose for the second time, it rose on a hornpipe.

The oldest frog couldn't fault the dancing, which was so vigorous that the musicians became slightly tearful in their efforts to keep up with it.

But as it moved into its final phase, he was startled to see that one frog was dancing backwards while the other six danced forwards. This was not at all a conventional hornpipe, and he feared it would end in disaster.

The frog dancing backwards was the little speckledy frog. Losing his balance, he clutched in turn at the frogs on either side, and they all collapsed in a pile.

The music stopped abruptly. One of the flute-players had the presence of mind to bring down the curtain so that the dancers could pick themselves up.

The oldest frog was quick to call out words of encouragement. "Bravo!" he cried. "Most original."

Now the flute players began to play once again, and their music was so sweet, so hesitant, so haunting, that the oldest frog felt a little shiver run straight through him.

The garden was full of magic when the curtain rose.

Softly, softly, light as leaves, the dancers were circling their stage.

They were stretching up high like willow trees and swaying from side to side. They were waltzing like frogs in a dream. As the music gathered pace, the dancers obeyed it, spinning and leaping in a dazzle of silvery green.

Faster and faster they danced, higher and higher they leapt, until they almost seemed to be flying.

Then at last the music began to dip and tremble and call: it was calling them forward to take their bows.

As the curtain fell, and the last note from the flutes died away into the midsummer night, the oldest frog sat alone under the stars. In the end, the ballet had been so much his favourite kind that he was hardly aware of where he was.

He sat as still as the very ground beneath him, half-remembering, half-dreaming of all the things that had happened during his long frog-life. He remembered many moonlit nights like this, from the time when he had been as young and green as a fresh spring leaf. He remembered many stories, many games of leapfrog and hide-and-seek. He remembered many ballets, performed here over the years on the great stone by the lake. He remembered his own dancing days, and his golden eyes gleamed.

One by one, the frogs crept round the curtain to the grassy hollow where he sat and settled round him in a circle.

"Did you like your ballet?" asked the little speckledy frog, leaning against him. "It was all on purpose, you know, those bits at the beginning."

The oldest frog only nodded, very, very slowly. He couldn't seem to keep his eyes open, and the little speckledy frog didn't like it.

"Where are you going?" he shouted
in the oldest frog's ear. "Wake up!"

The oldest frog jumped, but he didn't open his eyes. "Hush," he said in a voice that seemed to come from far away. "Don't make such a noise. It's all right. This is part of the ballet."

The little speckledy frog felt his heart turn over. "What do you mean?" he asked. "What's part of the ballet?"

The oldest frog thought for a while. "An old frog dozing off. An old frog drifting away. An old frog who won't wake up," he said. "An old frog dying is part of the ballet."

"Don't die," whispered the little speckledy frog. "I'm afraid of when the ballet ends."

By now the oldest frog found it hard to talk, but he knew he must. "You don't need to be," he whispered back. "Shall I tell you my favourite thing about the ballet?"

The little speckledy frog buried his face in the oldest frog's cool skin just as he had always done when things went wrong for as long as he could remember.

"My favourite thing about it," said the oldest frog, "is that it doesn't - really - end - at all."

Now all the frogs wanted to be close to him, and they gathered in.

All through the long night they sat with their oldest one. He would never say another word, and his great eyes would never open again, but he surely knew they were there, his family, as close to him as they could be.

Waking and dozing, dozing and waking by the oldest frog's side, the little speckledy frog knew he would want to cry quite soon, but he couldn't cry yet. Every time he found himself awake, he thought about what the oldest frog had said and wondered what it meant, but every time he closed his eyes he thought he knew.

For in his dreams he thought he heard the flutes play, and he thought he saw the curtain rise, and he thought he saw the oldest frog dancing, light and straight and graceful in the moonlight, dancing for all the world as if he would dance for ever.